BERYL'S BOX

To Jackie

First published in Great Britain by HarperCollins Publishers Ltd in 1993
First published in Picture Lions in 1993
Picture Lions is an imprint of the Children's Division,
part of HarperCollins Publishers Limited,
77-85 Fulham Palace Road, Hammersmith, London W6 8JB

Text copyright © Lisa Taylor 1993
Illustrations copyright © Penny Dann 1993
The author and illustrator assert the moral right to be
identified as the author and illustrator of the work.

A CIP catalogue record for this book is available
from the British Library.

ISBN 0 00 191309-3 Hb
ISBN 0 00 664288-8 Pb

Printed and bound in Hong Kong

This book is set in 18/24 Garamond

BERYL'S BOX

LISA TAYLOR Illustrated by PENNY DANN

Collins

An Imprint of HarperCollinsPublishers

Penelope Ponsenby was bored;

Beryl Bognut wasn't.

Penelope Ponsenby had five teddies, two pairs of roller skates, ten pots of luminous paint, three world cup footballs and a bike with special wheels for mountain climbing.

Beryl Bognut had a cardboard box.

Penelope's Mum and Beryl's Mum were the best of friends; Penelope and Beryl were not. Beryl didn't like the freckles on Penelope's ears and Penelope thought Beryl's legs were much too bendy.

But when Beryl's Mum went to visit Penelope's Mum, Beryl had to go too. She howled and scowled and bent her legs until at last she was allowed to take her cardboard box.

Penelope's Mum and Beryl's Mum sat and played cards and had a good time.

Penelope and Beryl sat and slurped milkshake – then used the straws to annoy each other.

Penelope stared at her teddies and her roller skates and her
luminous paints and her world cup footballs and her
bike with special wheels for mountain climbing.
She could think of nothing whatever to do.
Beryl put her cardboard box in
the corner of the room
and clapped and
cheered.

"What are you doing?" asked Penelope crossly.

"Shush!" said Beryl. "I'm trying to watch the football on the telly."

"That's not a telly. It's a cardboard box!" said Penelope and she kicked the box high into the air.

It did a huge somersault and landed SMACK! in the middle of the fireplace. Beryl was furious. She picked up the box and peered inside it. Suddenly she gasped.

"What is it now?" asked Penelope. So Beryl showed her the box. It looked very empty. "There!" said Beryl. "I knew you wouldn't be able to see them."

"See what?" asked Penelope.
"These sweets!" said Beryl.
Penelope peered even closer.
"They're for adventures!" she cried.
"They're for eating and having
adventures!" and she chucked
a sweet into the air and
swallowed it down in one.

Suddenly there was a sound – a sort of
gurgling and a splurgling – coming from
behind. Beryl spun round just in time to
see a great sploosh of water pouring down
the chimney. She jumped into the box.

"Quick!" she shouted.
"We'll use it as a boat."

The water rose higher and higher. It covered the floor, it covered the door. And the higher it got, the rougher it became, until a huge wave washed the box right out of the window and on to the open sea.

"Ahoy there!" cried Beryl, as an enormous ocean liner went sailing past. Penelope smiled and waved.

"Watch out for the sharks!" she said.

The boat sailed on and on.

"Look!" shouted Beryl. "There's land ahead." Penelope looked, then closed her eyes.

"It's an island," she said, "an island with big blue trees!" So they
started to paddle towards it.

Harder and harder, faster and faster they paddled. But just as they were about to land, they began to go round in circles.

"We're stuck in a whirlpool!" yelled Beryl. Penelope reached out and grabbed hold of a big blue branch on the edge of the island. Then she started to pull them in.

Beryl and Penelope sat down on the box. They were tired and very hungry. At the top of one of the big blue trees, they could see a bunch of big blue moon fruits. Beryl did one of her best bendy-legged jumps, but the fruits were too high up. So Penelope tipped the box on its side and leap-frogged on to the top of it. Reaching up, she chucked the moon fruits down.

Beryl and Penelope sat on the ground and munched the big blue moon fruits. They put the box in the middle and used it as a table. "I wonder what's on the radio," said Penelope, reaching out to switch the box on. "WARNING! WARNING!" came a voice, which sounded a bit like Beryl's, "HUGE GOOGLY MONSTER SPOTTED ROAMING MOON FRUIT ISLAND!" At that moment, Penelope felt something long and slippery slithering up her back.

"HEAARRGGHH!" The long slippery something was a long slippery tail, attached to a wide slippery body with a snaky slippery neck, on the end of which was a huge slippery googly monster's head!

There was the rumble and grumble of a gigantic hungry tummy, followed by a slurping burping sound. It was the huge googly monster – licking its sloppety lips!

Beryl picked up the box and swung it round three times before bashing the monster on its googly head. The monster bellowed, then went all cross-eyed and wobbly. With an angry roar, it stamped on the box. The box flattened out like a carpet.

"Quick!" shouted Beryl, jumping on top of it. "The magic words!"

"Bendy legs and ear freckles!" cried Penelope and she just managed to grab Beryl's hand as the carpet soared into the air.

Higher and higher they flew, until the monster was just a slippery speck in the distance.

And still they went on climbing – up and over the moon, then on past the stars which glittered cold and blue and hung like icicles in the sky.

They arrived back in Penelope's playroom just as Beryl's Mum walked through the door.

"Time to go!" she said. Penelope picked up the box and with a sad sigh handed it back to Beryl. "Same time next week!" said Penelope's Mum to Beryl's Mum. Beryl and Penelope smiled. Beryl thought that Penelope's freckles looked like yummy chocolate chips.

And Penelope couldn't help thinking that all the best legs must be bendy.

That night, Penelope's Aunt Caroline came round with a very late present for Penelope's birthday. Penelope ripped it open.

"WOW!" she cried, snatching the superest new computer from inside its box. "It's just what I've always wanted!" And throwing the superest new computer on the floor, she hugged the box tight to her chest.